Shopkins™

Once you shop...You can't stop!

LIGHTS, CAMERA, SHOPKINS!

By Meredith Rusu

W9-BSJ-971

Published by Scholastic Inc., *Publishers since 1920.* SCHOLASTIC and associated logos are trademarks and/or registered trademarks of Scholastic Inc.

The publisher does not have any control over and does not assume any responsibility for author or third-party websites or their content.

ISBN 978-0-545-94041-2

10 9 8 7 6 5 4 3 2   16 17 18 19 20

Printed in the U.S.A.   132 • First printing, 2016 • Book design by Erin McMahon

Scholastic Inc.

It's a brand-new day in Shopville. And Apple Blossom has BIG news for her friends.

"Have you heard?" she asks. "Lippy Lips is making a movie. She wants to cast a fresh face as the lead role!"

"What kind of movie is it?" Kooky Cookie asks. "I don't know," says Apple Blossom. "But it's sure to be this year's box office breadwinner!"

4

Everyone wants to audition . . . except for Strawberry Kiss.
"I'm not very good at acting," she says.
"Just give it your berry best!" Apple Blossom encourages her.

Soon the big audition day arrives!
"Thank you all for coming," announces Lippy Lips. "I'm looking to cast the freshest face in Small Mart. Only top-shelf talent will do!"

Apple Blossom auditions first. She acts out a scene from her favorite scary movie—*Night of the Living Cheese Monsters.* "*Hmmm,*" says Lippy. "Not bad, but a little too cheesy."

Cheeky Chocolate is up next. She auditions like an action hero!
"Hold on to your wrappers," she says. "This is going to be off the cart!"

8

Cheeky runs! She jumps! She shows off some semisweet karate moves!

"I've got this audition in the shopping bag!" she says.

"Very impressive!" says Lippy. "But a little too sugar-high energy for my movie."

Now it is Slick Breadstick's turn.

"Oh, ho, ho," he says. "I know just how to warm Lippy Lip's heart and win ze lead role!"

First, he sings a song: "The Microwave Power of Love."

Then he acts out a scene from the famous romantic film *Pride and Pre ju-dish.*

"That audition was simply delicious!" cries Lippy. "I've found my lead actor!"

All the Shopkins loved Slick Breadstick's audition!
In fact, perhaps they loved it a little too much . . .

13

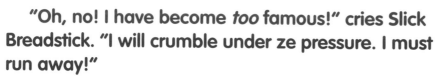

"Oh, no! I have become *too* famous!" cries Slick Breadstick. "I will crumble under ze pressure. I must run away!"

Lippy Lips sighs. "I guess the auditions will go on."

It is finally Strawberry Kiss's turn.

"I have high hopes for you," says Lippy Lips. "You'd be the perfect sweetie pie for my movie."

Yikes! Now Strawberry Kiss is *really* nervous!

To juice herself up, she tries out funny poses. *Maybe Lippy Lips wants to produce a comedy,* she thinks.

But Lippy Lips is *not* impressed. "Too silly," she says. "Again."

Strawberry Kiss tries to mix it up. She pretends to be a damsel in distress.
"Too hammy," says Lippy Lips. "Again."

18

Strawberry Kiss tries acting scared.

She tries acting spoiled.

She even tries acting like frozen fruit.

"No, no, no!" cries Lippy Lips. "None of this is right for my movie!"

"Um, what *are* you looking for?" Apple Blossom asks Lippy Lips. But before Lippy Lips can answer, Strawberry Kiss starts to cry. All this pressure has really jammed her up!

Everyone is impressed with Strawberry Kiss' audition.

"That's perfect!" Lippy exclaims. "Finally, just the acting I need for my movie: *A Tale of Two Aisles*. It's the tragic love story of a produce romance gone sour. A real tearjerker! Strawberry Kiss, the lead role is yours!"

"I can't believe it!" says Strawberry Kiss.
"I knew you had it in you," cheers Apple Blossom. "And now, we'll get to check you out on the big screen!"